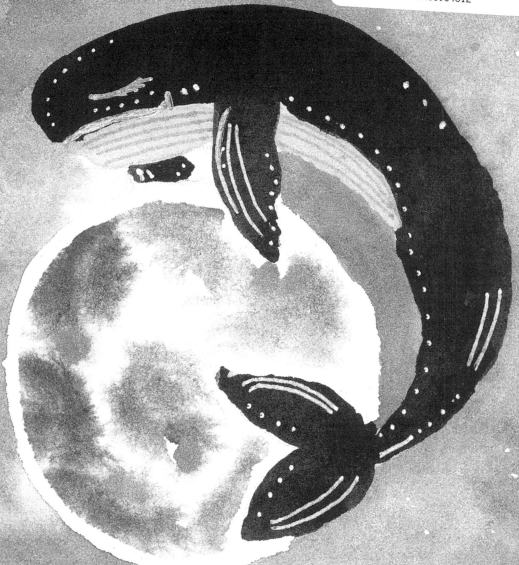

The Whale, the Moon, and the Stars
For the Adventurous Child

DEBORAH ECHERMAN

To order additional copies of this book, contact:
Xlibris
AU TFN: 1 800 844 927 (Toll Free inside Australia)
AU Local: 0283 108 187 (+61 2 8310 8187 from outside Australia)
www.xlibris.com.au
Orders@Xlibris.com.au

ISBN: Softcover   978-1-6641-0411-2
         Hardcover   978-1-6641-0413-6
         EBook   978-1-6641-0412-9

Library of Congress Control Number: 2021904521

Print information available on the last page

Rev. date: 04/13/2021

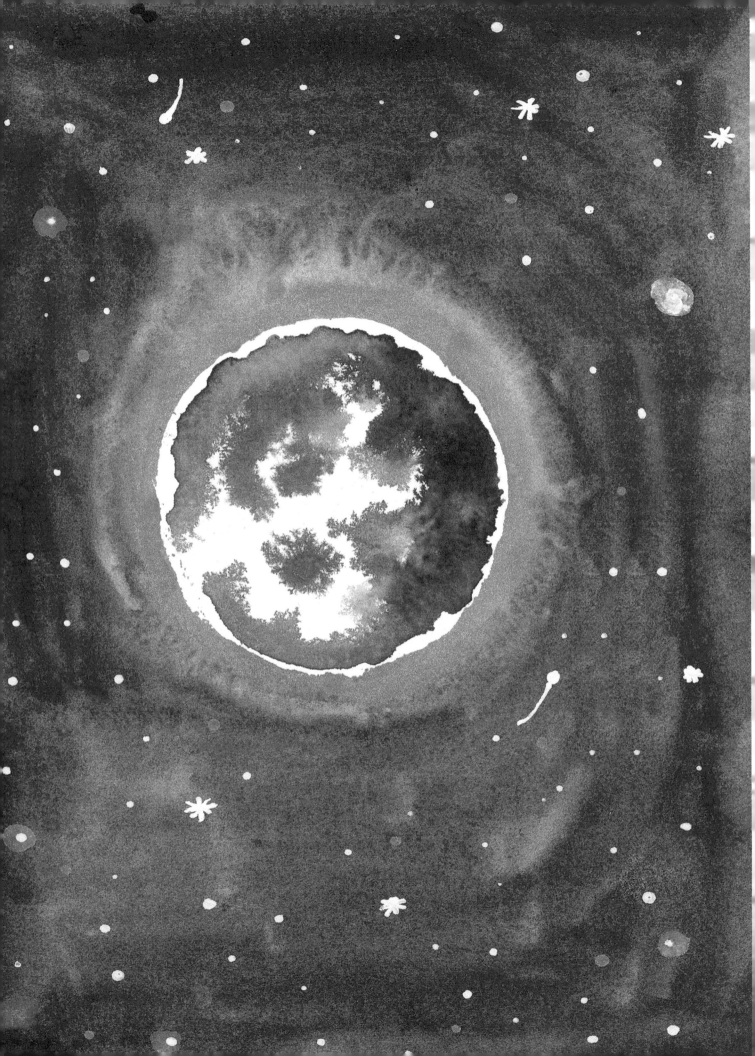

Have you ever noticed that sometimes, when you are riding with your mum and dad in the car or walking with your friends at the park, the moon seems to follow you everywhere you go? It does not matter where you go; she is always there.

As a kid I used to think that she was my friend, and I used to have long conversations with her.

One day, Dad told me that the moon was not following me. He said that the moon was very far away and that it appeared to follow me because objects that I passed by, such as trees and houses, were very close in comparison. As people walk or drive along in the car, things that are much closer to us appear to move between us and the moon.

I felt very embarrassed about thinking that the moon was following me, but Dad told me I was not the only one to be confused about that. Then he told me a story about the whale, the moon, and the stars.

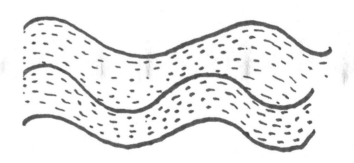

One day, a young whale named Kobie, saw a big, shiny object on the surface of the water while swimming in the ocean. It was something the whale had not seen before, as she never used to swim alone at night. This shiny object was beautiful, and it seemed to move along the sky next to the whale.

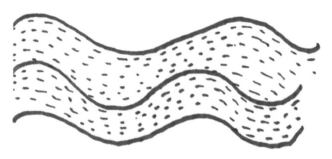

She tried to go near the surface. She wanted to ask this shimmery thing why it was following her. Could they be friends?

Once on the surface, she could not find it anywhere—until she looked up above in the sky.

Above the surface of the water, the glow was even stronger. Kobie was amazed, and the whale spent the whole night just looking at this shiny, beautiful thing. She tried jumping out of the water to see whether she could reach it, but she could not. By daytime, her soon-to-be friend was already gone.

The whale swam along her neighbourhood, asking different sea creatures whether they knew what this light-catching object was. Kobie asked the wisest creature she could think of, the crab, who told her that object was the moon.

The wise crab told the whale that the moon lived in the sky and that it only came out at night, when the sun went to sleep.

Kobie was so excited to hear about her new friend that she left the crab's cave very fast; the crab did not have time to tell her that the sky had no limits. Reaching the moon was very difficult.

The whale decided she needed to go to sleep as soon as possible so she could be wide awake at night to see her friend.

For many weeks, she spent countless hours at night telling the moon her deepest secrets and dreams.

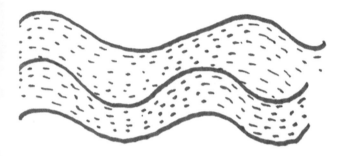

The only thing the whale could think about was the next time she would see the moon. Her love for the moon grew so much that she stopped spending time with her family and friends and doing other things she enjoyed.

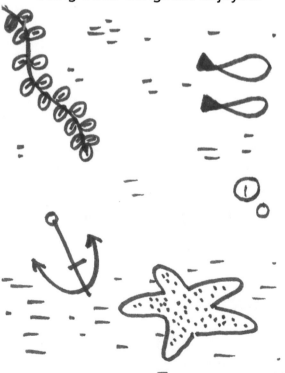

During the few hours of the day that the whale was awake, she was unhappy. Her mum and dad constantly complained about her relationship with the moon. The whale also thought, *I give so much of myself to the moon. She knows everything about me, and I know so little about her … Maybe I just need to get closer.*

So Kobie decided she needed to find where the moon lived. Maybe that way they could be together for ever. And then they could know everything about each other.

One night, while Kobie's mum and dad were deeply asleep, she took off on a journey to find her beloved friend.

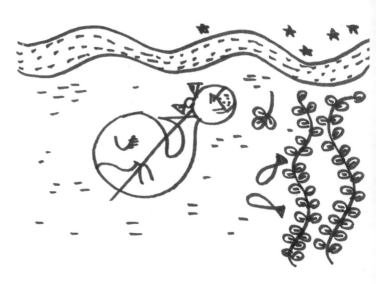

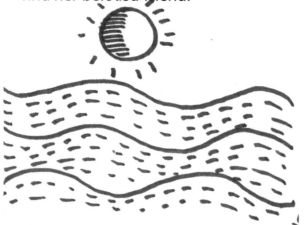

The whale swam and swam, as far as she could go, to the corner where the sky meets the sea. No one know how far away it was; it was unknown to every single creature on earth.

Kobie was very scared of reaching that corner, as many creatures believed that was where the earth stopped, and if you went there, you might fall off into the outer space. She did not know what outer space was, but it sounded scary. To distract herself and to guide her journey, she sang soulful songs, as many whales do. And she wished the moon listening.

Her journey took her to very cold waters, where huge ice crystals floated on the water's surface. She had heard of this place. It was called the Arctic.

When the whale realised where she was, how far she had gone, how alone she was, and how she was nowhere nearer to the moon, she got very sad.

She cried a lot; she missed her family very much, and the idea of living with a friend who did not return her love seemed pointless. Worst of all, she was lost and did not know how to go back home.

In the distance, she saw some creatures that looked like something from a fairy tale. As she got closer, she could not believe it. They were narwhals! She had heard of them before, but she thought they were made up for the bedtime stories her mum use to tell her when she was a calf.

If the narwhals lived nearby, maybe they could tell her the best way to get home.

She watched them for a while, trying to find the best way to explain to them how and why she ended up there. Kobie was ashamed of her story; she felt she was a fool for falling into the moon's tricks. But she filled herself with courage and decided to ask for help.

As she swam towards these mystical creatures, she said to herself, *You are very brave for doing things even though you are scared.*

When the whale was close enough to the narwhals, she introduced herself and told them her story. They were impressed that such a young whale could swim so far by herself. The narwhals then told her that sometimes you can love someone very much, but the other object might not love you back the way you want. But that does not make them bad.

They also told the whale that her friend the moon only had eyes for the sun. The moon and the sun loved each other very much, and every day one of them had to die to give life to the other one. A few times during the year, they can come together in an event called eclipse.

Then the narwhals explained to Kobie that the moon was very complicated, with different phases. Some nights you could see a full moon, while on others, you'd see just half or a bit less than a full moon, called a gibbous moon. Then there were nights when the moon was so sad about not seeing the sun that she did not come out at all, called a new moon. The whale had noticed that, but she did not understand why.

Everything made sense now. However, there was still one question to answer. "How do I get back home?" she asked.

The narwhals replied, "All the answers you seek are in the sky. You were so worried about trying to get to the moon that you did not even see the stars!"

"What does that mean?" the whale asked, confused.

The narwhals said, "The stars hold the spirits of great adventurers and explorers; the best ones are brighter than the others, or else they make groups called constellations." Using their long teeth—which looked like unicorns' horns—the narwhals drew the most important constellations on the sand.

They explained, "Depending on where you are, you may see different constellations that can help you find your way. In the south, you will see Orion, called the hunter, and the Southern Cross. In the north, you will see Ursa Major and Ursa Minor, called the big bear and the little bear. Can you see the constellations?"

Kobie answered, "Yes, I can see them, but I do not understand how that will help."

The narwhals giggled and said, "They will help you find north. Because the northern sky is above us, you need to find big and little bear constellations. On the tip of little bear's tail, you will find Polaris, the North Star. Follow her, as many other explorers before you did, and she will take you home."

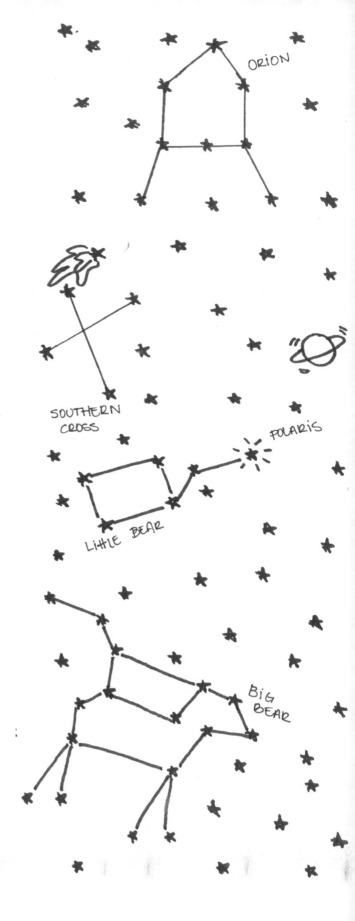

Before going back home, the whale wanted to know more about the sky at night. Her new friends then told her the story of the aurora borealis—the Northern Lights.

According to a Finnish legend, the aurora forms when Arctic fire foxes run through the sky so fast that their large, furry tails brush up against the mountains and create sparks that light up the sky. Many explorers chase these mythical foxes, as they believe that catching them will bring them money and fortune. Then the narwhals said, "See my friend, you are not the only one who has gone a long way to find something in the sky!" That made the Kobie laugh.

It was almost midnight, and the narwhals were happy that their new friend was so interested in their stories; they decided to tell her another, the one about the Milky Way.

The name Milky Way might make you think of dairy products in the sky, but the Milky Way is not made out of milk; instead, it is made of many, many stars.

Even though it is a huge group of stars, it is not a constellation like the ones we have told you about before. It looks like a band of faint light crossing the sky, consisting of countless distant stars.

In Maori mythology, the Milky Way is related to sharks and rays. These animals are considered guardian spirits. According to the legend, a huge shark called Te Māngrōa was placed in the sky by the demigod Māui to protect the Maori tribes on earth.

Another Maori legend says that the god Kiho-tumu formed a ship in the heavens and sailed across the sky. This ship was named the *Long Shark* by the Maori people, and they believed the ship was there to protect them.

The whale could not believe there were so many stories about the night sky and that different cultures believed in such different things.

She asked the narwhals for one more story before going home, so they told her the story about one of the most famous meteor showers in the sky, the Perseid meteor shower.

The meteor shower is named for the Perseidae, who were the sons of the ancient Greek hero Perseus.

Perseus was a very important Greek hero; he even has a constellation named after him. Perseus was known for many epic adventures, such as fighting and defeating the scary Medusa, a terrible monster that could look you in the eyes and turn you into stone.

The Perseid meteor shower was related to Perseus's rescue of Princess Andromeda. Andromeda was abandoned by her parents on a rock by the ocean to pacify a sea monster. Perseus found her and saved her. They fell in love with each other and had seven sons and two daughters.

Because the constellation Andromeda is just next to the Perseus constellation, the Greeks believed that the meteor shower was from Perseus and Andromeda's children.

It was almost daytime. "Time flies when you are having fun!" the whale said.

It was time to go home. Before she left, the narwhals told her to go to the surface so that she could see the sunrise, or dawn. "It is the colourful way the sun shows his love for the moon when they are giving life to each other. When it happens at nightfall, it is called sunset or dusk. The Romans believed that the sunrise was created by Aurora, goddess of the dawn, renewing herself each morning and flying across the sky to announce the arrival of the sun."

The whale was amazed by all the beautiful shades of orange, red, yellow and pink and textures of the sky, . She did not know such stunning thing could happen. Her journey had brought her lots of new knowledge and understanding about the universe.

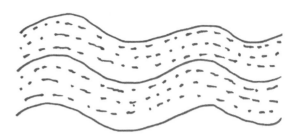

The narwhals very kindly guided the whale outside the Arctic waters. Once in the open ocean, they said goodbye.

On the whale's journey home, something incredible happened. It was daytime, but suddenly the sky became very, very dark, as if it was night-time already. It was so dark that it was difficult to see what was in front of her.

Then, Kobie remembered the narwhals' story about the eclipse and thought, *This must be an eclipse!*

As the two celestial figures passed close by one another, she felt very happy that the sun and the moon got to see each other that day.

She watched the eclipse until it was over. After that, she swam back home. It was a very long way, and by the time she arrived, it was time to go to sleep.

The whale went to bed, fell asleep and almost immediately had a wonderful dream. She was up in the sky, swimming in between all the stars. She saw the fire foxes creating the aurora borealis and the great shark protecting the Maori people, and at the end she became part of the night sky.

As my father finished his story, he said, "Do not feel bad about not knowing everything. Be like the whale—excited about learning from your mistakes, and always be ready to learn something new. Do not be disappointed about not reaching the moon; you might land on a pretty cool star."

CPSIA information can be obtained
at www.ICGtesting.com
Printed in the USA
BVHW020505160721
612047BV00002B/42